WHO
STOLE THE APPLES?

SIGRID HEUCK

A DRAGONFLY BOOK · ALFRED A. KNOPF
NEW YORK

This is a

One  and another

and some more

make a big green

Deep in the  is a 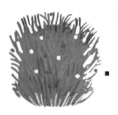 .

In that same  stands a

 . Behind the  grows a

big  . And nearby lives

a

In the autumn the  fall from the 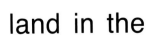 . The  fall, too, and land in the . Then the  eats 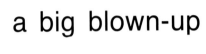 until his tummy is as round as a big blown-up

But one bright sunny autumn morning, all the were gone. There wasn't even one left on the , though the evening before each had been full. There wasn't even one lying in the . This made the unhappy. But then he realized that don't just go away by themselves, and he decided to find out who had stolen them.

"Good-bye, dear !" he called.

"Good-bye, dear 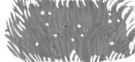!" Away trotted the

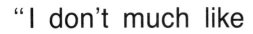. In the  he met

a . "Who stole all my ?

Can you tell me?" asked the . "Well,

I didn't take them," answered the .

"I don't much like . But early this

morning, I saw something flying by. It might

have been the thief."

"Thank you," said the .

At the edge of the  he met a little

. "Who stole all my ? Can

you tell me?" asked the .

The  shook his head. "No, but I did see

something fly over the 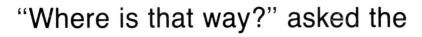," he said.

"Which way was it going?" the asked.

"That way," growled the .

"Where is that way?" asked the .

"If you let me ride on your back, I'll show you!"

said the  . Then willingly the

took the little on his back. They went

over a and across the ,

by some and then

past a . In town they met a ,

,

,

and .

Whenever the  didn't know which way to turn, he would stop and ask, "Now where?" "That way," the little would growl, showing him the way. But suddenly they could go no farther, because they had reached

the big wide

"We will have to find a  to take

us across the now," said the little

 . A  was docked nearby.

"We are searching the world for some stolen

 ," the  said to the  .

"We need to cross the  now. If you will

take us across, we will give you an

on our way home," promised the .

"One  won't be enough for my  ," said the  .

"In that case, we will give each one an

," promised the  .

"I certainly hope we'll have enough," growled the

 . The  agreed to take them, and

they all set off in his  across

the wide  .

After a long voyage they arrived in a land where the ☀ was always shining, and there they met an 🐘. "Who stole all my 🍎🍎? Can you tell me?" said the 🐎. The 🐘 thought a minute. "Something flew by me earlier," said the 🐘

"They were not . They were not . Perhaps they were . Go ask the . He knows everything."

The thanked him and promised him

an 🍎 as a reward.

They searched until they found the .

"My  were stolen away. Have you

seen them?" asked the . "Oh! That

explains why the  have

been making so much noise lately," said

the . "Please tell us where the

are," pleaded the . They followed

the  to a and on every

was a . Each was holding an

 in its beak.

The  saw the and and cawed in fear. But it is impossible for to caw without opening their beaks. All the tumbled down to the ground, and quickly the little gathered them up. "Thank you for your help," said the to the , and they gave him an as a reward.

At last the  and the little started

for home. As promised, they gave an to

the . They gave one to the

and one to each

. They passed by the

, who had been busy

laying dozens of white . All the

had gone home

for dinner, and the

had dinner in their .

The ran beside them part of the way. The were being milked. The had taken a bath and was resting on the green in front of his . By this time the had set, so the was dark, and the was nowhere in sight. "He told me he doesn't much like ," said the . "I'm glad," growled the little .

They made their way back to the in the in the big . They had brought back with them only , one for the and one for the . The rest had all been given away.

"Please don't worry," the said. "Next autumn, when the fall from the , there will be many more. You can come visit me. We will eat so many that our tummies will be as round as big blown-up ." "Wonderful," said the . "See you next year!"

SIGRID HEUCK was born in Cologne, Germany, and now lives in the Bavarian Alps. She has illustrated many books for children but is best known for *Who Stole the Apples?* which has sold more than half a million copies in fourteen languages since its publication in 1977.

DR. M. JERRY WEISS, Distinguished Service Professor of Communications at Jersey City State College, is the educational consultant for Dragonfly Books. Currently chair of the International Reading Association President's Advisory Committee on Intellectual Freedom, he travels frequently to give workshops on the use of trade books in schools.

A DRAGONFLY BOOK PUBLISHED BY ALFRED A. KNOPF, INC.
Translation copyright © 1986 by Alfred A. Knopf, Inc.
Illustrations copyright © 1977 by K. Thienemanns Verlag, Stuttgart
All rights reserved under International and Pan-American Copyright Conventions. Published in the United States by Alfred A. Knopf, Inc., New York, and simultaneously in Canada by Random House of Canada Limited, Toronto. Distributed by Random House, Inc., New York. Originally published in Germany as *Pony, Bär und Apfelbaum* by K. Thienemanns Verlag, Stuttgart. Copyright © 1977 by K. Thienemanns Verlag, Stuttgart. Translation first published in hardcover by Alfred A. Knopf, Inc., in 1986.

Library of Congress Cataloging-in-Publication Data: Heuck, Sigrid. Who Stole the Apples? Translation of: Pony, Bär und Apfelbaum. Summary: Relates the adventures of a horse and a bear as they try to discover who has stolen the apples from the apple tree that grows in a forest clearing. [1. Apples—Fiction. 2. Horses—Fiction. 3. Bears—Fiction. 4. Rebuses] I. Title. PZ7.H438Wh 1986 [E] 86-2977 ISBN 0-394-88371-3 ISBN 0-394-98371-8 (lib. bdg.)

Library of Congress Catalog Card Number: 86-2977
ISBN: 0-394-82623-X (pbk.)

Manufactured in the United States of America   1 2 3 4 5 6 7 8 9